To Max
I hope you enjoy this
book. I've gotten to know
the real Frisky and he is
quite a character.
Lynda

Jeffrey J. Mann

Frisky and the Booba La Bobba La

Words and illustrations
By J. J. Mann

Frisky was a Saint Bernard puppy who was born on a farm. He wasn't the smartest, fastest, or most anything dog, but there was something special about him. Frisky was too young to care.

He was excited when a man and a girl
took him to a new home. Here his life
would be interesting and adventurous.

Soon he was sniffing everything in his
way when thought he saw a strange
looking bird. But it wasn't a bird, it
was a Fairy. To Frisky, she looked like
a sparkly little girl with wings, and she
had a stick with a light on the end.
Before he could sniff her, she flew
away.

Being special doesn't mean he was always good. As a puppy it was his duty to create a little trouble sometimes. One day he met the neighbor's cat, and another time he pooped in their flowers. Other than a few naughty moments, he was likeable and cuddly.

Today's adventure was exploring the
lake. A shy little girl was watching.
While checking out a boat, he put his
front paws on the boat, and left his
back paws safely on the pier. This
pushed the boat away from the pier,
and suddenly there was a splash and
Frisky was floating in the water. That's
when Frisky learned to swim.

Back at home, he noticed the little girl.
As she went around the yard smelling
the flowers, Frisky followed her. She
said "I love flowers. They look
beautiful, and they smell pretty."
Frisky agreed they looked beautiful,
but if they had a little more "stink", he
thought they would smell better.

Suddenly the little girl hit a tree branch and fell. As she sat on the ground, she said "I've always been clumsy, but everyone tells me I make up for it because I'm so smart." Before Frisky could ask who she was, she flew away. Frisky hoped he would see her again.

By the time he was six months old,
Frisky weighed almost 100 pounds. As
big as he was, he was still afraid of
worms and bugs and anything icky.

He enjoyed playing with the cell
phone. When he tapped on it with his
nose it would play funny music, and
sometimes he could hear little people
inside the phone talking.

He also took a lot of selfies.

Fall came and there were new things to do. He helped rake the leaves.

He helped carve pumpkins.

And he attacked the scarecrow.

The dog next door was a German
Shepherd named Rex. One stormy
night he told Frisky that he needed to
hear about the Booba La Bobba La.
Frisky was worried.

Rex started telling an evil story, and Frisky was so scared he ran into the closet. A sheet fell on top of him, and it wouldn't come off.

Frisky backed out of the closet, and began to howl. When Rex saw this, he figured Frisky was gone, and the Booba La Bobba La was now after him!

Rex was so scared that he ran so fast that only his legs were moving.

When Rex got home, he hid under the bed.

The next day Frisky went outside.
While he was sniffing, the little girl
flew up to him, wiggled her finger
telling him to come, and said she
needed his help. Then she flew into the
woods.

Deep in the woods, she flew into a
cave. Frisky followed. The light on the
little girl's stick lit the way. Inside the
cave, they went higher and higher.

When they came out, everything was covered with snow. Frisky had never seen snow before, but he loved the cold. He walked, and rolled, and even ate the snow.

The little girl flew over to a beautiful castle made of ice. When Frisky tried to lick it, she stopped him. She told him her name was "Booba La Bobba La", but he could just call her Boo. So the Booba La Bobba La was not a scary monster after all.

Boo had lived in the ice castle her
whole life. Today, a mean sorcerer
with a dragon was going to come, and
the dragon's fiery breath was going to
melt her house. Boo wanted Frisky to
save her. Frisky was afraid, he didn't
know what he could do.

Boo tapped him on the nose with her stick and suddenly he was small enough to fit inside the castle. Then they waited inside.

Soon they saw the sorcerer and his dragon. Boo and Frisky went outside. The sorcerer was a little man, but the dragon was a terrible looking beast. Frisky was worried. What should he do now?

Boo bent over to tap Frisky on the
nose to make him large again but she
dropped her stick.   Frisky wanted to
run away, but he knew he couldn't
leave Boo alone.

He ran around the dragon in circles so
the dragon's breath couldn't burn him.

Boo ran behind the sorcerer and called Frisky. Frisky ran behind the sorcerer too.

When the dragon came over, Frisky jumped out and chomped on the dragon's tail as hard as he could. The dragon ran away. Boo picked up her stick and tapped Frisky on the nose, making him big again.

The sorcerer was scared, but Boo made
him sign a treaty saying he would
never bother her again. Then he left.

Boo told Frisky he was special, and kissed him on the nose. Frisky was so excited that he licked her back. After Boo dried off, she took him home.

Frisky heard his owner calling, and ran over to him wagging his tail. "Where have you been, you silly dog"? I was fighting dragons and saving a little girl, Frisky thought to himself. And although he didn't know it, he was beginning to grow up.

The End

Jeff Mann is a retired engineer, the often exasperated owner of a Saint Bernard puppy and a teller of children's stories. He has won art awards at local and state competitions, and he is currently studying creative writing at Waukesha County Technical College. When not taking care of his dogs, he is renovating a house, sailing canoeing and kayaking. Winter finds him at the ski hill where he teaches skiing and snowboarding. In his spare time, he plays the banjo, and played in a band for 10 years, both locally and at Bluegrass festivals.

Frisky is the hero of the story and my one year old Saint Bernard puppy. His real name is Whiskey, but I changed it for the story. Most of the puppy pictures in the book, are from pictures of him taken on my cell phone. Frisky's personality and adventures (other than the fairy and dragon) are actual happenings.

Made in the USA
Lexington, KY
21 August 2015